D1573107

IS FOR VAMPIRE

EMISSARIES FROM THE DEAD

THE THIRD CLAW OF GOD

V IS FOR VAMPIRE

Z IS FOR ZOMBIE

IS
FOR
VAMPIRE

An Illustrated Alphabet of the Undead

ADAM-TROY CASTRO

ILLUSTRATED BY
JOHNNY ATOMIC
OF LEAGUE ENTERTAINMENT

HARPER Voyager
An Imprint of HarperCollinsPublishers

This book is a work of fiction. The characters, incidents, and dialogue are drawn from the authors' imagination and are not to be construed as real. Any resemblance to actual events or persons, living or dead, is entirely coincidental.

V IS FOR VAMPIRE. Text copyright © 2011 by Adam-Troy Castro. Illustrations copyright © 2011 by League Entertainment, Inc. All rights reserved. Printed in the United States of America. No part of this book may be used or reproduced in any manner whatsoever without written permission except in the case of brief quotations embodied in critical articles and reviews. For information address HarperCollins Publishers, 10 East 53rd Street, New York, NY 10022.

HarperCollins books may be purchased for educational, business, or sales promotional use. For information please write: Special Markets Department, HarperCollins Publishers, 10 East 53rd Street, New York, NY 10022.

FIRST EDITION

DESIGNED BY PAULA RUSSELL SZAFRANSKI

Harper Voyager and design is a trademark of HCP LLC.

Library of Congress Cataloging-in-Publication Data has been applied for.

ISBN 978-0-06-199186-8

11 12 13 14 15 LPR 10 9 8 7 6 5 4 3 2 1

For Bela

—Adam-Troy Castro

For Suzanne

—Johnny Atomic

 # Is for Arterial Spray

Let's get this much out of the way first.

To vampires, you are nothing more than an attractive candy wrapper. Your contents are under pressure and may be opened any way they please: a bite in the neck, a slit along the wrists, or even in some cases a plastic tube, siphoning away goodies to be stored in a blood bag that can be taken out and enjoyed later, like cold pizza. You may be in love with one and you may think that sucking your life away is just their way of demonstrating deep affection, but let's be honest here: even the farmer with a soft spot for his favorite cow isn't really interested in more than the quality of the milk.

Some ladies adore the vampire when he's posing in the moonlight, or going on about the children of the night, or even when he's inserting those fangs of his into the soft expanse of their throat. But the vampire has the most affection for you when you're hemorrhaging. That's why he chooses the throat. There's a major artery there; punctured, the spray achieves some stellar distance.

Or to put it another way, frat boys have a favorite party trick that involves shaking up a can of beer, stabbing it with a pen, and then guzzling the brew as it explodes through the hole. They think this is funny for some reason. We won't argue the point. But put that frat boy in a tuxedo, and give him a V-shaped hairline, and put spooky organ music on the house stereo, and put a feminine neck in his mouth instead of a can of Bud, and . . . well, he still doesn't seem very continental, does he?

B Is for Bedroom

She languishes alone in a four-poster bed, on the third floor of a dark, drafty mansion. Her hair is long and her lips are moist and she lies beneath white silk sheets, dreaming of a phantom lover who has haunted her nights with promises of unchecked passion. It is past midnight when she hears the tapping on the glass: a rhythmic, insistent tattoo that first brings a frown to her beautiful features and then prompts her eyes to flutter open in confusion tempered by yearning.

His shadow stands framed by the window, backlit by moonlight. Three stories up, with no ledge to support him, there is no easy explanation for his presence; even the most likely approach, a ladder, can't account for the way he bobs up and down, as if stirred by the same errant breezes that wrap the tendrils of fog around his aristocratic costume. His features are lost in blackness, but the overwhelming impression is of youth, and vigor, and powerful sexuality.

"Invite me in," he whispers. "Invite me in."

Watching as if from a thousand miles away, she sits up, sets the sheets aside, and glides, rather than walks, to the window.

He has to do this kind of thing every night, because powerful as he is, he's not allowed to enter private homes unless he's invited.

But since few of his victims seem capable of refusing the strange guy who wants in through the window in the middle of the night, that's pretty much a formality.

So why bother having that rule at all?

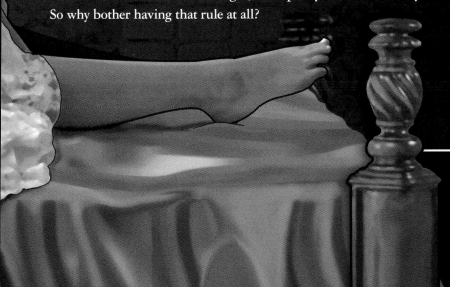

C Is for Children of the Night

He is carrying a candelabra up the stairs of his gloomy old castle when he pauses in midstep, struck by the sudden howl of a wolf in the distance. "Ahhhh," he says portentously. "The children of the night. What music they make."

This is the unlucky houseguest's first clue that the fellow in the tuxedo is more than a little bit creepy.

But we know what he is, and so we have a number of questions.

Since this is his home, and he has dwelt here as a member of the undead for, literally, centuries, he has no doubt heard those howls several times a night, every night, since before Columbus first dipped his toes in the Caribbean. Is he really that surprised, that impressed, every single time the children of the night bay at the moon? Does he really call attention to it every single time it happens?

Why didn't it get old for him sometime after, say, his second or third century?

Is for Dracula

You know those vampires who were actually pretty decent people in life, then became evil, slavering predators upon being turned? The ones that make the wise old vampire hunter warn their grieving loved ones, "Don't listen to anything Bob tells you, because that's not Bob anymore"?

Vlad Tepes, also known as Count Dracula, also known as Vlad the Impaler, was not one of those vampires. During his lifetime, his castle was often surrounded by the writhing bodies of his enemies, impaled on stakes and praying at length for the sweet release of death. This was, we remind you, in front of his house. Most mass-murdering despots don't want their bloody atrocities cluttering up the immediate neighborhood; they give the orders and they receive the reports but they don't feel any pressing need to be reminded of yesterday's brutal whim every time they stand on the parapet, enjoying the view.

Dracula was different. He impaled people at his dinner parties, he impaled people on his lawn, he impaled people just because he felt like it. He didn't get that nickname because it was catchy. For him, a day without impaling people was like a day without sunshine.

So, naturally, somebody had to go and make him a vampire, on top of everything else.

This is the supernatural world's equivalent of the worst person in your office being promoted to supervisor.

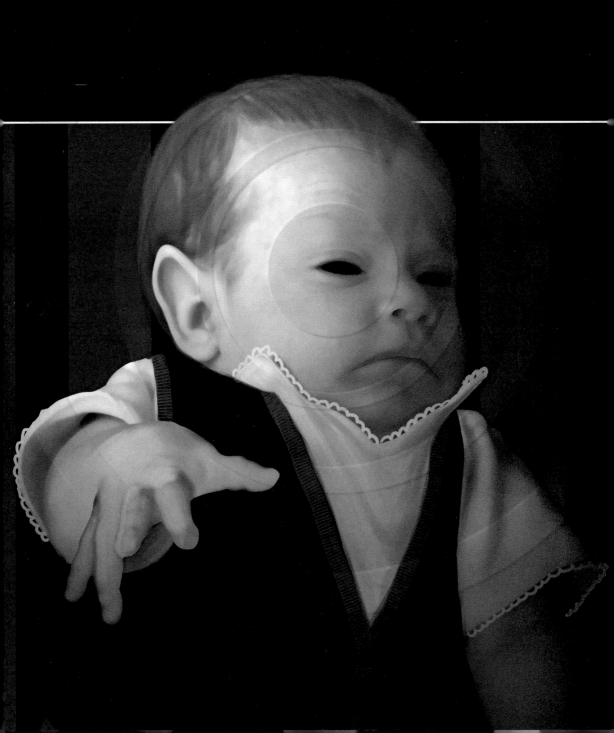

 **Is for Eternal Youth**

According to most accounts, people who get turned into vampires remain the same age forever, which is a great deal if they're twenty and at the peak of their physical attractiveness, less so if they're some decrepit, doddering eighty-year-old. Children who get turned into vampires continue to mature emotionally but not physically and retain the whininess you would expect from people who will never be taken seriously as adults, no matter how knowledgeable they might be about the music or fashion trends or obscure political movements of centuries past.

But it could be worse.

Imagine being turned into a vampire as an infant. You may grow up intellectually, develop the conversational skills of a true bon vivant, and even become a deadly killer in your own right, but you will always need somebody to carry you around and dress you and powder your backside and push you around in your coffin pram. You will hear all the other vampires celebrating their dark rites in their all-night bacchanals from the imprisonment of your crib, waiting for somebody to come and feed you pureed RH-negative from a little jar. Unlike you, that will get pretty old. Your only hope for some semblance of dignity is to be lucky enough to turn, and forever command, a wet nurse, who can do all your stalking and biting for you and return full of fresh corpuscles by your nightly feeding time.

But you better hope she doesn't get staked one night while she's out. Because you'll be in for a long wait.

 Is for Fear

Imagine the intrepid band of vampire hunters, skulking through the crypt in search of the fiend who's been terrorizing the countryside. Their hearts pound like trip-hammers, reminding them that they're still alive. They know that this may be their last night on earth . . . at least as the people they want to be. And then one whispers, "Look!" He points to the top of the stairs, where the dark figure stands, not caught sleeping as they had hoped, but fully awake, fully refreshed, and ready to kill. His eyes glow red, like wounds.

The chill in the air seems to dip another thirty degrees.

This is the terrible thing about fighting vampires: it's impossible to man up. However many you track to their respective lairs and stake, however many you see reduced to ash by the first beam of sunlight streaming through a break in the clouds, you will never be able to conquer that first jolt of fear.

Being in the presence of a vampire is a lot like being a small scurrying thing minding its own business when it suddenly senses the shadow of an owl passing in front of the moon. Every instinct tells you that you have no chance. Every instinct tells you to freeze or to run. Every instinct tells you that you have no business being there.

But you are there. And so is he.

Might as well make the best of it.

Is for Garlic

It tastes great on bread and tortellini. But vampires are reputed to harbor a powerful allergy to the stuff, one that sickens them and sends them fleeing in search of less aromatic environs. And so people who suspect vampirism in their neighborhoods stock up, hanging bulbs of the stuff from their windows and draping it from their bedposts and even, in extreme cases, wearing it around their necks.

But what if all the myths and legends are fake?

What if some vampires got together one fine night, drunk on some inebriate they just drained in an alley, and started giggling over how stupid and gullible we are? What if they started regaling one another with all the stupid things we could be induced to believe?

What if one, barely able to get the words out without snarfing, said, "Hey, you wanna do something hilarious? Send Renfield down to the village tavern promoting the rumor that we hate garlic! Fake a few twitching fits around people who have the stuff around the house, and by the end of the week all the pretty girls will go to bed at night wearing garlic necklaces! It'll get into their sheets and into their hair and they'll lie awake for hours trying to ignore the smell and walk around the next day positively stinking of the stuff!"

"Nice one, Varney."

"I can almost picture that! So funny!"

"Too bad even mortals couldn't possibly be that stupid."

Worse, what if garlic doesn't actually repel vampires? What if it actually attracts them?

Vampire party tricks suck.

H Is for Hypnotism

You know that sensation of vertigo you get when you're standing at the edge of a bottomless drop and make the mistake of looking down? The main reason it's so disconcerting is that you can feel it pulling at you. You know that stepping forward means tumbling head over heels to a bone-shattering splat, but the tug is undeniable, and you pull back one heart-thumping moment later, knowing that you shouldn't have looked.

Making eye contact with a vampire is a little like that.

When you meet the eyes of another human being, you might feel the urge to look away, or you might feel some personal magnetism drawing you in, but there's still a real-world limit to how much the mere gaze can affect you, without words and deeds and personality backing it up. But meeting the eyes of a vampire is a little like looking into that bottomless pit. You're so used to seeing a human soul when meeting another person's gaze that the failure to sense one right away only tempts you to look deeper and focus harder until you've already lost your balance and fall all the way in, which makes you suggestible when the immortal bloodsucker intones, "Call me . . . master."

What makes experienced vampire hunters so resistant? They don't have to stare. They know they won't find anything. They understand that looking into a vampire's eyes is a lot like looking into the black marbles that fill the head of some dead animal preserved through taxidermy. A vampire's eyes are like Toledo. There's no *there* there . . .

I Is for Inconsistent Rules

Dracula walks around in the daylight. He does. Read Bram Stoker's account. Dracula ambles along in the middle of the afternoon, wearing no protection greater than a big floppy hat. Other vampires sparkle in the sun. Yes, really. Like sequins.

Holy water kills vampires, except when it doesn't. Sometimes you throw holy water on a vampire and he just laughs at you.

Vampires can turn into bats. Except that some can't. Some will happily tell you that the bat stuff is just Hollywood being Hollywood. Wolves, maybe. Except maybe not.

And, of course, we've already covered garlic. It may be proof against vampires. And it may just be an odiferous fashion accessory.

Pretty much every vampire story ever told contains a prominent scene where somebody, either vampire or vampire hunter, has to go over the rules one more time, to let you know which ones apply and which ones don't in that particular case. Some vampires delight in telling their opponents how everything they've heard up until now is wrong. Crosses? "Sorry, no. That's just a myth." Mirrors? "Don't be ridiculous, how do you think I always manage such impeccable grooming?" Running water? "Same answer." Sunlight? "Well, it hurts, but only because I'm also a redhead." Stakes through the heart? "Yes, that would kill me, but it wouldn't be the healthiest thing in the world for you, either." At which point the intrepid vampire hunter has to say the hell with it and pull out a hand grenade.

Don't assume anything, because we're beginning to suspect that the people who tell the stories are just making stuff up as they go along.

Is for Just Some Goddamned Cat

You're back with your band of fearless vampire slayers, skulking through the cemetery in the dead of night. You have reason to believe that the Count is in the immediate vicinity. For all you know, those wisps of fog rolling in over the gravestones might even be him, waiting for the perfect moment to strike. You know that you risk not only your life, but also your immortal soul. Your nerves are on edge.

Then you catch a glimpse of two inhuman eyes glowing in the dark just up ahead. The breath catches in your throat as the night is pierced by a high-pitched yowl.

A creature leaps . . .

. . . and of course, it's just some goddamned cat.

This is not a phenomenon limited to vampires. It doesn't matter what you're searching for in the darkness. It can be anything from a masked serial killer at a summer camp to a slimy alien in a spaceship. There will always be some goddamned cat, waiting for the moment when you're most ready to jump out of your skin, so it can leap out at you, yowling. They live for that crap. Lord knows why.

About the only positive aspect of this phenomenon is that you can always count on the monster following behind it by about five seconds.

So here comes the count.

Followed by the Count.

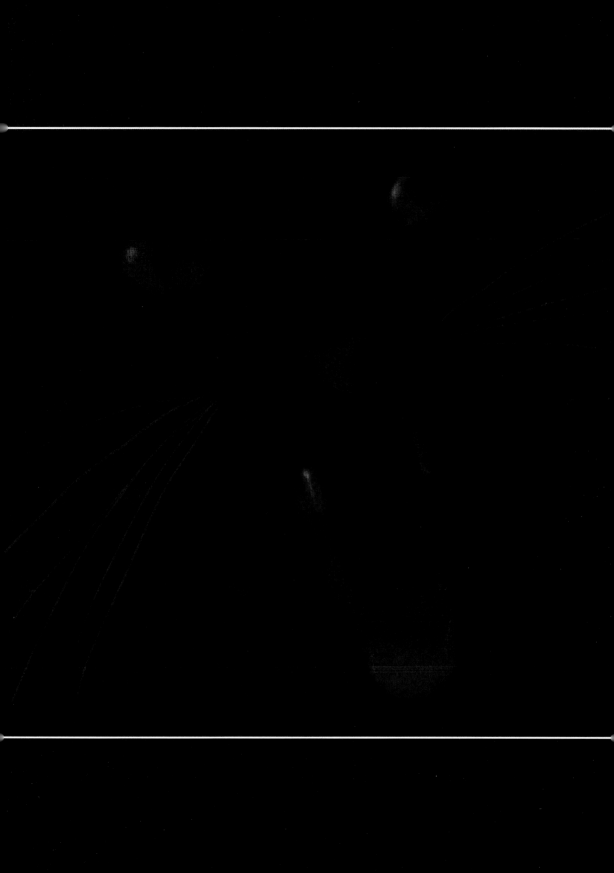

Is for Kiss of the Vampire

Being stabbed in the throat shouldn't be any fun. It should be one of life's least pleasant experiences. And yet, to those of us who get visited by the undead in the middle of the night, the bite carries an undeniable erotic charge. The gasp of pain goes along with the gasp of pleasure, one so irresistible that the victim longs for the fiend to return the next night and the night after that.

Why?

Do vampires prey on an exclusive diet of masochists? That would explain a lot. It would account for the beautiful woman who always sleeps alone and unfulfilled and hopes that somebody will come along and perform the equivalent of jabbing two hypodermic needles in her neck. And two nights later, after she's been warned that another bite will mean eternal damnation, the same woman is positively turned on by the very prospect.

We suspect, however, that with their dietary limitations, vampires might have had a little trouble arranging regular meals at some points in history. Not so much today. Today they'd only need the Internet or the classified ads in the back of their local alternative weekly.

It's more likely that the fangs don't just draw blood but also inject something else: a euphoric of some kind, something that immediately floods the brain with endorphins and makes anything that happens an orgasmic pleasure. Such a drug would also compromise your ability to make rational life-or-death decisions, especially if its effects linger . . . which, frankly, also explains a lot.

If so, we learn another lesson.

You should not get bitten by a vampire and drive.

 Is for Life

If they were fortunate enough to get turned at the right stage of life, with the right kind of renewable income, enough anonymity to get away with nightly predation, a warm place to rest their immortal heads, and neighbors who can provide regular sustenance without also providing a steady stream of pitchfork-wielding mobs, being a vampire almost seems like a pretty good deal. All you have to do, if the majority of accounts can be trusted, is give up sunlight and certain Italian foods.

But don't you believe it.

We're living. We can surprise ourselves. We can meet people we've never met before and know that they like us because we charmed them with our words, not our eyes. We can spend time, daylight time, on the beach in Jamaica. We can go to the water park. We can decide to get out of that rut we've fallen into. We can try new restaurants. We can have kids. We can make silly faces in the mirror. We can drink wine. We can get a stateroom instead of having ourselves shipped. We can even look our age, and if you think that sucks, try socializing when you look seventeen years old and can't understand the appeal of any music that's been written since 1563.

And if that's not bad enough:

Imagine living so long that having a bad decade is about as unremarkable to you as a human being would find having a bad day. Imagine being in a bad mood for a *century,* and imagine how many *years* your friends would have to spend snapping you out of it.

There's absolutely no charm or romance in being *young* and crotchety.

Doesn't seem quite so romantic now, does it?

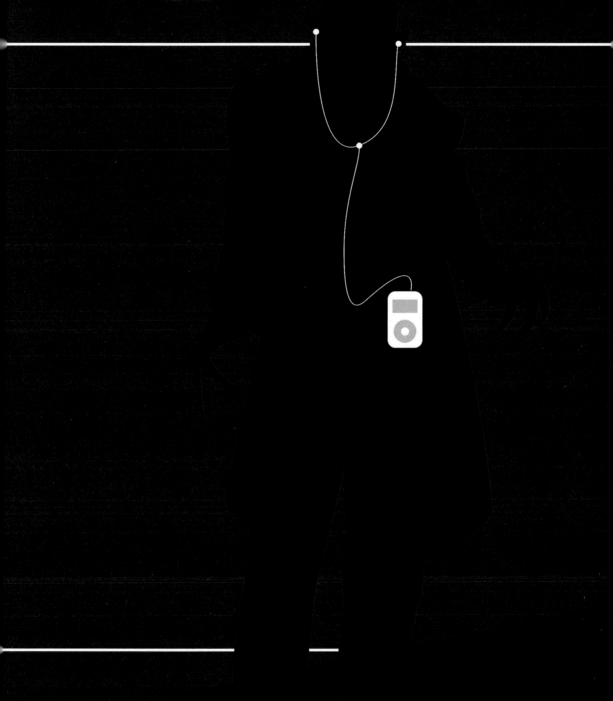

iVlad

 Is for Mirrors

Again—and we cannot possibly stress this enough—accounts differ. This may be true or it may be another urban legend. But some folks claim that vampires don't show up in mirrors.

Track down the rationale and you'll find that it has to do with silver. Vampires receive no love from the silver backing that makes mirrors reflect or from the silver nitrate on common photographic film.

Fine.

But this is no longer a limitation now that we've had the digital revolution.

These days, if you're a vampire who wants to see what you look like, it's downright easy. Get a webcam. The real-time image is as good as any mirror could possibly be, and you'll be able to straighten your tie or touch up your realistic flesh-tone makeup without suffering any drawbacks from your condition. You'll even be able to snap a screen capture and send it to your uncle Vlad in the old country.

As for photography, much of that is done with pixels now. You can take as many pictures of yourself as you like.

This will open up entirely new career opportunities for the average vampire. Imagine an athletic, vital, sexually magnetic movie actress who never gets any older, who doesn't have to take the grandma roles even if it has been fifty years since she first played the high school cheerleader.

The studios would love to invest in somebody like that, as the next star of the—please excuse the expression—silver screen . . .

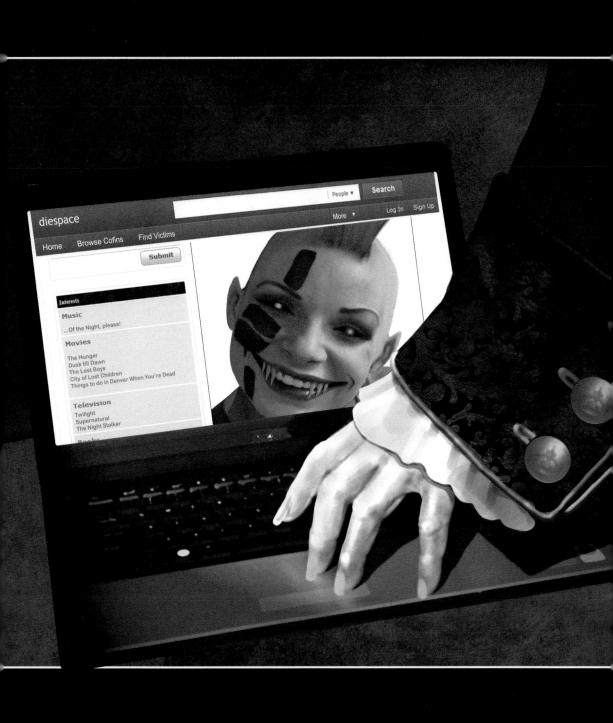

Is for Night

Vampires and their human apologists love to wax poetic about the glories of the night. They'll go on and on about the terrible dark beauty of the night, the cold purity of the night, the way the woods only come alive during the night, the way a victim's throat looks so pale and inviting during the night. There are some vampires so enamored with using the word *night* that you couldn't make a decent drinking game out of taking a shot every time they used the word. It would be fun to start, but you'd get sick or pass out or both within five minutes.

Why do vampires go on like this? Well, in part, because they know how to say it. A proper vampire saves the word *night* for the end of a sentence, dragging out the "igh" in the middle until it comes close to sounding like an orgasm. They raise their eyebrows at you and say, "I am . . . the Count. I rule the niiiiiiiiiiight," investing that one drawn-out syllable with every possible flavor of sensuality and menace. In some extreme cases, just their delivery is enough to make sufficiently susceptible victims think, "You know, that sounds pretty good. I might as well allow myself to be bitten. It'd be almost worth spending all my daylight hours in a coffin if I can rule the niiiiiiiiight like that."

But . . . we all know people who have only been on one real vacation in their entire lives, and not even to someplace all that exotic, but to a simple tourist destination. They come back from this trip telling you about all the great things they saw at, say, Enchanted Acres. They show you endless pictures taken at Enchanted Acres. And as the trip fades farther and farther into the past, they continue to fixate on those four days and five nights at Enchanted Acres. It's not that Enchanted Acres is all that special a place. It's that they have nothing to compare it with and nothing else worth talking about.

Similarly, vampires go on and on about "the magic of the niiiiiiiight" because for as long as they've been vampires they haven't tasted the magic of midmorning or late afternoon. It's a function of what they're used to. If they were awake only between 8:00 and 8:15 P.M., they'd be just as eloquent about the glories of that one quarter hour. "I ruuuuuuule 8:07."

Thanks a lot.

Is for Being Caught
Outside at Sunrise

For beings who supposedly dissolve into a puff of smoke at the first ray of sunlight, vampires are certainly sloppy when it comes to keeping track of time.

We've all seen the implacable vampire hunter cornered in a dark room by the undead monster he's been stalking. Things look grim. But then the vampire hunter rips the curtains off the big picture window, and the rays of the sun stream in, setting the fiend ablaze like a roman candle.

Somehow, the vampire's always surprised.

This is bad enough when he's caught at home, minding his own business, but vampires almost always look just as astonished when they're caught out in the middle of a field somewhere, miles and miles from home, and get nailed by the first shaft of golden light that appears over the horizon.

This makes no sense. The sun doesn't exactly prowl around in tennis shoes, sneaking up on people. One can almost imagine some protector of vampires coming up with some way to put a belled collar around the sun's neck, so it can't approach in silence.

It seems to us that beings who immolate when exposed to sunlight should keep better track of the time.

And they probably do. The smart ones, at least.

Any vampire caught out in the middle of a field when dawn breaks is an incompetent at his chosen deathstyle and deserves the inevitable consequences. The ones who survive past their first night ought to learn to anticipate sunrise, to know exactly when they should expect it, to know that they should be in the coffin and taking their daily rest long before the horizon starts to glow.

So if you really want to keep track of possible vampires in your neighborhood, then get yourself a list of subscribers to the *Farmers' Almanac.*

P Is for Parcel

Address changes present the average vampire with a number of unique challenges. As Dracula demonstrated, they can't just get up and go. They have to hire a real estate agent to find a suitable abode sufficiently shielded from the sun, arrange shipment within a sealed crate, and have themselves unpacked on arrival. This is a pain in the rump even under the best of conditions and presupposes that the crate won't fall out the back door of somebody's delivery van and break open in the middle of the road at high noon. But even that's not the worst that could happen.

Imagine one Baron Alucarus, shipping himself from the family manse in the old country to a creepy, decaying mansion last owned by a Wisconsin cheese magnate. But transpose just two digits on the shipping order and his crate ends up at a holding facility in Miami. There it sits, untended, while the baron molders inside, wondering why his faithful servants have not arrived to release him.

After six weeks, the mistake is discovered and the crate is moved out to the loading dock for reshipment. Except that it's now in direct sunlight, and enough ultraviolet gets through to make the poor baron give off a little vapor through the slats. This is spotted by an alert employee who wets the package down with a hose. This obliterates the address marked on the side, necessitating the crate's relocation to a lost packages facility.

It is not excavated for almost six weeks, at which point new staffers wonder if an inspection will help them determine its proper destination. And so they take crowbars to the crate and pry it open, right there in the sunlight.

Meanwhile, the baron's human servants can only watch sadly as the mansion he'd purchased is repossessed for delinquent mortgage payments.

Is it seriously any wonder that vampires endure sticking around those decaying, cobweb-festooned old mansions?

It's safer than moving.

 **Is for Quiver**

Those who want to get into the vampire-slaying business will find few items of inventory as indispensable as the common, garden-variety crossbow. It's not just that vampires are vulnerable to stakes in the heart and a crossbow is a fine way to deliver death at a safe distance, far from those fangs, claws, and hypnotic eyes. That, of course, is a plus. More to the point, a vampire who's just been disturbed after centuries of imprisonment in a tomb will recognize it and quite possibly fear it. Confront another vampire who hasn't been around to watch the march of technology while wielding an Uzi stocked with silver bullets, and you'll likely get nothing worse than a puzzled scowl before he pounces.

Better yet, the creative vampire slayer knows that crossbow shafts are capable of carrying a variety of useful payloads. Fire, for instance: those black capes go up like something that's been dipped in kerosene. You can also wrap the shafts in pages from the Holy Bible, carve a variety of religious symbols into the points, and deliver explosives for the occasional vampire who you feel needs a more pyrotechnic end.

Variety's the key. Prepare your quiver with a wide assortment and keep trying different things until you finally find something that works.

Of course, it probably still won't be enough.

But wouldn't you rather have ten chances than just one?

R Is for Rising

The worst ordeal for any novice vampire hunter is the vigil beside the coffin of a fallen loved one as you wait for them to rise.

You can't just drive the stake into the corpse's chest now and be done with it. You have to wait until your loved one sits up in the coffin and turns to look at you. No moment in the vampire-slaying business is more dangerous, because there's a certain degree of rejuvenation involved, and your loved one will never look more vibrant, more perfect, more glowing with life. Mildly pretty women will now look like sirens; reasonably handsome men will now look like gods. This will not be minimized by the poor lighting in most crypts. They'll glow with their own light, and everything you ever felt for them will be magnified by an order of ten.

Sometimes they'll say your name.

This is when you're supposed to push them back down into their coffin and stake them.

It's not just self-preservation—it's concern for their immortal souls. You don't want them to rise as ravenous, bloodthirsty things, damned to prey on the living. You want them to move on to their just rewards in heaven. So ignore their cries and their attempts to fight back and drive that stake through the heart, knowing that you did the right thing.

Or, at least, hoping you did.

After all, hospital patients are sometimes revived after being pronounced dead.

Maybe that heart you just pulverized was still beating all this time, only too faintly for you to hear.

Maybe the scene that just took place here was not you saving your loved one's soul; maybe it was you jumping to the wrong conclusion and damning your own.

Seriously.

Whatever you do end up doing, you'd better be sure.

S Is for Seductive

You've got to say this about vampires: they certainly know how to score. They have to.

Oh, sure, the men are reputed to be sophisticated, soft-spoken, and urbane, the women shapely, seductive, and saucy; they maintain eye contact long after anybody else would turn away and instead lean in close, whispering suggestions tempting enough to overcome the objections most people have to allowing the penetration of their jugular veins.

If you're at all tempted, on any level, the vampires have probably already won. They're players.

And again, this is because they have to be. It's not like they have anything else to recommend them. They're dead. They're cold to the touch. They require you to keep to their schedule instead of respecting yours. Some accounts say that their breath stinks like rotting meat, and not just in the morning. Many of them are hung up on demanding your absolute obedience. If you come to your senses and try to break up with them, they become stalkers. And, frankly, as lovers go, they make the most selfish human bed partner who ever lived look like a paragon of giving. Think about what you say to a lover who's driving you up the wall with self-centered behavior. That's right. "What do you want from me? *Blood?*"

Well, yes.

The vampire has to be seductive. Because otherwise, the vampire's no prize.

T Is for Tombs for the Budget-Conscious

The need for shelter drives many vampires without ancestral mansions to less aristocratic refuges, and by that we don't mean only crypts and mausoleums. We've also read about vampires spending their days in sewers, in subway tunnels, in deconsecrated churches, in mine shafts, in parked vans, and in the dark crawl spaces of suburban homes.

It seems clear from all this that economic realities remain with us after undeath. If they're not titled royalty with some drafty old castle to knock around in, they have to make do. That means they don't get to wander sepulchrally up and down their entrance stairs, issuing spooky declarations about the music made by the children of the night. Their actual homes might offer no more elbow room than the average old-fashioned phone booth.

This seems grotesquely unfair.

We therefore suggest a reasonably priced alternative.

Vampires without independent wealth, but with a little money for a down payment, can rent a backhoe and bury a mobile home. Once the dirt is patted down the lot will look vacant; but for the hatch nobody will ever feel any pressing need to investigate. The vampire in residence will have a bedroom, a living room, plenty of space to house guests willing and unwilling, and best of all, no need for an additional coffin—for what is that arrangement but a big buried box?

Is for Undead Rules

How do you quantify undeath? It's not life. It's not death. It's been called both and neither. It's also been described as a blessing and as a curse, often in the same sentence, as if even considering the question leaves the questioning one wandering around in endless circles. But is it really that hard to describe?

Undeath is being trapped on a hard wooden bench at the railroad station, watching other people board trains when you know you have no other place to go.

Undeath is that vacancy at the pit of your stomach that lets you know you're hungry, when you also feel queasy and know that anything you try to eat is going to leave you feeling sick.

Undeath is that formal dinner three hours after all the interesting guests have run out of topics of conversation, when the most doddering person at the table begins a story you've heard before.

Undeath is a doctor's waiting room where you sit hoping for the inner door to open even though you know that it never will.

Undeath is remembering what it was like to visit better places in happier times and to know that nostalgia can only torture you, because you'll never be anywhere that special again.

Undeath is Scranton.

See? Was that so hard?

Is for Van Helsing

It ultimately all comes down to him: the learned professor who recognizes a vampire's work in the symptoms of the waning young ladies, who overcomes the skepticism of those around him and forms the intrepid band that will turn the hunter into the hunted. Abraham Van Helsing is everything his immortal nemesis is not: kind, elderly, selfless, and wise. He should be overwhelmed by the vampire's vast supernatural resources, but if anything, it's an even match.

Every vampire has a Van Helsing. Sometimes it's a descendant of Van Helsing. At least once in recent times it's been a silly guy with a sword and a musket with no apparent relation who used the name anyway. Trust us, that one wasn't *the* Van Helsing.

Sometimes the Van Helsing is someone who doesn't pretend to be *the* Van Helsing and doesn't even use the name but plays the same role. He's just a guy who happens to be a walking encyclopedia about all the myriad ways to kill a vampire and who's loud enough and insistent enough to soldier on in the face of all the skeptical resistance until he finally talks all his potential allies into joining him on his trip to the mausoleum, when every rational impulse would lead them to pack their things and get the hell out of town instead. The Van Helsing can be counted upon to get at least a couple of them killed in the attempt, but they follow him anyway, because he's the Van Helsing, and when all is at its bleakest he's the one guy who at least sounds like he knows what he's doing.

In some extreme cases, the first battle between vampire and vampire hunter takes place when the Van Helsing's young, and the war continues in fits and starts for decades until the Van Helsing is old and wrinkled and suffering joint pain. On such occasions there's always a moment when the vampire, who hasn't aged a day in all the intervening years, cruelly mocks the Van Helsing for really letting himself go.

This is never a good idea, because it's at precisely that moment that the Van Helsing rams the stake home.

Never make fun of a Van Helsing for being old.

Like fine wines, Van Helsings only improve with age.

W Is for Wolves

Some vampires can transform into wolves. They do this only when they feel like it, or when the trick comes in handy, such as when they're confronted with determined vampire hunters and need to leap out of a high window before bounding off into the night.

This is not to be mistaken for the ailment suffered by that other supernatural creature known as the werewolf. Most werewolves transform without volition. They burst out of their clothing and romp around the woods all night long, only to wake up in the morning with a pounding headache and the awareness that they need to find a convenient clothesline with garments that fit them before they wander sheepishly back into town. For werewolves, the whole business can be described only as a mortifying inconvenience.

This does not seem to be true of the vampiric version. Vampires turn into wolves when it suits them and turn back when it suits them. Many older vampires seem to have also mastered the trick of conveniently absorbing their fine clothing at the same moment, only to have it reappear on their backs without so much as a wrinkle when they reclaim their human shape—a neat trick, establishing that while they may be hell on any innocent virgins, they are certainly less of a threat to the neighborhood dry cleaner.

Werewolves are entitled to resent vampires a little bit because of this. And many do. The original wolf man, Lawrence Talbot, is reputed to have hunted Dracula across the continents. But was this because he was fed up with the fiend's reign of terror? Or was he just irritated at the superior attitude of the guy who didn't have to buy a new, unshredded suit every thirty days?

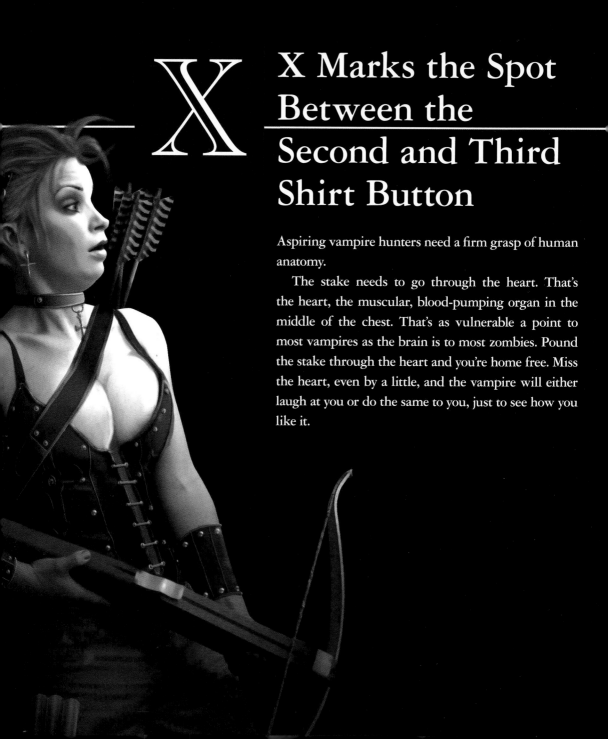

X Marks the Spot Between the Second and Third Shirt Button

Aspiring vampire hunters need a firm grasp of human anatomy.

The stake needs to go through the heart. That's the heart, the muscular, blood-pumping organ in the middle of the chest. That's as vulnerable a point to most vampires as the brain is to most zombies. Pound the stake through the heart and you're home free. Miss the heart, even by a little, and the vampire will either laugh at you or do the same to you, just to see how you like it.

Learn where the heart is. Practice on dummies if you have to. Draw yourself diagrams. Grow so adept at identifying it that you can hit the bull's-eye even in the dark, because that's exactly the skill set required. That subterranean crypt with all the cobwebs is not going to have track lighting. There'll be torches, if you're lucky. The shadows will be dancing and your tension level will be peaking and it'll be hard as hell just to keep your hands steady enough to hit the top of the stake with the hammer, let alone ram the point into its proper position. The target's not that large, and you can run into all sorts of trouble going in at the wrong angle and allowing your stake to get deflected by the ribs.

Do it wrong and the vampire will open his eyes and say, "Ummmm . . . that's my duodenum." And nobody wants that.

Y Is for You'll Never Defeat Me, Mwa-ha-ha

One of the many things that keeps vampires from taking over the world is their insistence on first telling us, at length, how powerful they are. The average vampire spends so much time telling Van Helsing and his mob that they're nothing that they have time to drape the windows with garlic, paint a fresco of crosses on the coffin lids, load their crossbows with flaming arrows, and fire from a dozen angles. If the vampire would just shut up and attack then the slayers would be toast, but instead he must describe how many enemies he's defeated, how many kingdoms he's seen rise and fall, how easily he'll break their limbs like twigs, and how he could, if he chose, kill every single one of them with the merest twitch of his vampiric fingers. Some vampires are so very much in love with the sound of their own voice that they then waste even more time with crazed maniacal laughter, as if afraid that somebody, somewhere, isn't paying enough attention.

Why do they insist on sabotaging themselves in this manner?

Well, it may be that they're dead and therefore have trouble recognizing that their long harangues amount to a waste of breath. Or it may be that they've spent so much time wandering their vast ancestral castles with nothing but the tapestries for company that they just appreciate having somebody to talk to.

In the end, the key factor that saves us all may be that vampires are . . . lonely.

Z Is for Zealotry

And yet the vampire hunter is no better. Get the average vampire hunter off on a tangent and you're in for a fine evening's rant about the evil at loose in the countryside, about the obscene beasts who walk among us, about their status as perversions of life, about how God (often pronounced as "Gott") wants us to defend the souls of the unwary against the things from beyond the pit.

Granted, much of this goes along with the job description. A vampire hunter needs to be able to recruit allies and won't be able to rev up his crowd by selling the task at hand as just another tiresome chore. To a vampire hunter, tracking the bloodsucker to his lair is a holy calling, a summons from the Almighty, a quest that reduces all of mankind's other endeavors to the level of a dithering hobby. There's no room for nuance. There's us, and there's them, with no room for common ground in between.

The other vampires we've heard about, the benign ones who don't really want to hurt anybody and who try to treat their undead state as just another medical condition to be managed with the help of willing donations and occasional trips to the blood bank, the ones who just want to mind their own business and let you mind yours, get cut no special slack. To the dedicated vampire hunter, these well-meaning vampires are abominations as well.

Look at it that way and you'll see that the vampire hunter may not be an intrepid crusader on our behalf but just another self-righteous prig who really ought to go get a life and is too inflexible to worry about nuance.

Read enough history and you'll learn that we've suffered far more at the hands of that kind of guy than we ever have from vampires.

So maybe that's the best lesson we can learn from all this. Maybe the true battle between good and evil has nothing to do with daywalkers and nightwalkers, odd dietary requirements, or immortals with sun allergies. Maybe, for those of us who just get on with our days and nights, the common enemy is not alive or dead, mortal or immortal, living person or vampire.

Maybe, just maybe, the folks we all need to keep an eye on are the fanatics.

Channel 8 Public Access Presents

Now: The Vampire Menace
8:00 Wight Supremacists
8:30 X-treme Makeovers

This book could not have been completed without constant input from the Triple-A Manuscript Folding Service and Stir-Fry Bonanza of Madison, Wisconsin; the Lee Van Cleef Memorial Vicious Sneer Early Warning Hotline; my good friend Michael Burstein, whose sole joy in an otherwise lonely and deprived existence is finding his name in the acknowledgments of books he didn't have anything to do with; Bela Lugosi, who deserved better; more seriously Charlaine Harris, who generously provided kind words despite the manuscript's multiple digs at "her" kind of vampire; the various members of the South Florida Science Fiction Society Writer's Workshop; editor extraordinaire Diana Gill; associate editor Will Hinton, who worked harder on this book than he should have had to; agents Joshua Bilmes and Eddie Schneider of the Jabberwocky Literary Agency; my wife, Judi, who is even now rolling her eyes in dismay at the trouble I get into writing acknowledgments; miniature horse Dakota, who drew blood from Judi's fingertip once and was therefore as close as she ever got to genuine vampire; and my friend and collaborator Johnny Atomic, who in addition to providing illustrations of triumphant spookiness and beauty also spent several weeks field-testing our new line of garlic-scented aftershaves, to the substantial and lasting chagrin of his wife, Shelley Jackson. If you belong here and I left you out, I apologize. Cowabunga.

Johnny Atomic

Ken Chapman	League Entertainment
Maria Chapman	League Entertainment
Jason Torres	League Entertainment
Rob Westerfield	Westerfield Studios
Diana Gill	For laughing out loud
Will Hinton	For leaving nothing out
Richard Aquan	For working it out
Jabberwocky	For getting it out
Larry Aramanda	For loaning it out
Mike Hill	For anything I missed
John Perry	For standing around
Christian Palamaro	For the Long Trip

Special Thanks

Kris Renta
Courtney Nawara
Gabriel Jackson
Julian Jackson
"Blue"

Gratitude

Adam and Judi Castro

ATOMIC V CASTRO

(writer) is an internationally acclaimed author of fantasy, science fiction, and horror. He has been nominated for two Hugos, five Nebulas, and two Bram Stoker Awards, his most recent award nomination being the Stoker nod for his terrifying novella *The Shallow End of the Pool*. His seventeen books include the science fiction thrillers *Emissaries from the Dead* and *The Third Claw of God*. *Emissaries* won the Philip K. Dick Award. Adam lives in Miami with his wife, Judi, and a motley assortment of cats that includes Meow Farrow and Uma Furman. Readers interested in finding out more about his projects can check out his website at www.sff.net/people/adam-troy.

(artist) is the cofounder of the wildly successful concept house League Entertainment. He is the cocreator of the popular Choose Your Doom interactive story series as well as the Simon Vector comic book series.